Swamp Monsters Don't Chase Wild Turkeys

There are more books about the Bailey School Kids!
Have you read these adventures?

Swamp Monsters Don't Chase Wild Turkeys

by Debbie Dadey
and
Marcia Thornton Jones

illustrated by John Steven Gurney

A
LITTLE APPLE
PAPERBACK

SCHOLASTIC INC.
New York   Toronto   London   Auckland   Sydney
Mexico City   New Delhi   Hong Kong   Buenos Aires

No part of this publication may be reproduced in whole or in part, or stored in a retrieval system, or transmitted in any form or by any means, electronic, mechanical, photocopying, recording, or otherwise, without written permission of the publisher. For information regarding permission, write to Scholastic Inc., Attention: Permissions Department, 555 Broadway, New York, NY 10012.

ISBN 0-439-33338-5

Text copyright © 2001 by Marcia Thornton Jones and Debra S. Dadey.
Illustrations copyright © 2001 by Scholastic Inc.
SCHOLASTIC, LITTLE APPLE PAPERBACKS, THE ADVENTURES OF THE BAILEY SCHOOL KIDS, and associated logos are trademarks and/or registered trademarks of Scholastic Inc.

12 11 10 9 8 7 6 5 4 3 2 1   1 2 3 4 5 6/0

Printed in the U.S.A.   40

First Scholastic printing, October 2001

*To Maria Barbo — a great editor
who is wonderful at chasing
writing monsters!*

Contents

Swamp Monsters Don't Chase Wild Turkeys

1

Swamp Dread

"Kick it!" Eddie yelled to Howie. Howie kicked the empty soda can back to Eddie.

"I can't believe all this trash," Liza said, shaking her blond ponytail and kicking another can. The kids were in Bailey City Park on a sunny November afternoon.

Melody picked up a can and tossed it into a trash can. "People are pigs when they don't throw away garbage."

Eddie pulled off his ball cap and snorted. "I'm a pig. Snort. Snort," he teased.

"Very funny, pig breath," Melody sneered. "Let's watch these guys play football."

"Awesome," Eddie said. "Maybe they'll

1

let us play." The four friends sat down at the edge of the field. A group of adults tossed a football back and forth. One very tall man with green spiked hair and green sunglasses kicked the ball really hard.

Liza shook her head at Eddie. "These guys are way too good for us," she said. "We'd get hurt."

"Not me," Eddie boasted. "I can slam a ball with the best of them."

"Watch out!" Howie shouted. The ball blasted toward the kids and Melody had to duck to keep from being hit. The tall green-haired man didn't waste a second. He let out an ear-piercing cry and ran straight toward the kids. Melody, Howie, Liza, and Eddie scattered in four directions just in time.

"That was a close call," Liza said as the man raced past them.

"What was he screaming?" Eddie asked.

"I don't know," Melody said. "But that ball is heading toward Swamp Dread."

Liza shivered. No one ever went into Swamp Dread. Ever. Vines and weeds made it a tangled mess, not to mention the trash that people had dumped there. Liza thought Swamp Dread had to be the creepiest place on Earth.

"Where did that guy go?" Howie asked when the green-haired man didn't come back.

"Maybe a swamp monster gobbled him up," Eddie joked.

"That's not funny," Liza said. "You shouldn't kid about things like that."

"Liza's afraid of swamp monsters," Eddie teased.

"I am not," Liza said, putting her hands on her hips, "because there are no such things as swamp monsters."

Eddie stood up and walked toward the swamp. "How can you be so sure there aren't swamp monsters? After all, the muck at the bottom of Swamp Dread is perfect for growing strange things — like monsters."

Liza's face turned pale, but Howie patted her on the shoulder. "Don't worry. The only things at the bottom of Swamp Dread are decaying plants."

Liza seemed relieved, but Melody looked worried. "Do you think that guy needs help?" Melody asked. "I hope he didn't get lost in the swamp."

The four kids wandered over to the edge of the swamp, kicking trash and cans out of the way. "I don't understand," Liza said. "Why would people throw their old paint cans and underwear in the swamp?"

"That's easy," Eddie said, "because they don't want them anymore."

"No kidding," Liza said. "What I meant was, why don't they put them in trash cans?"

"They're pigs," Eddie said, snorting.

"I'm not worried about trash," Melody said. "I'm worried about that!"

2

One Big Puppy

"Look at those," Melody said, pointing to the mud near the swamp.

Howie squatted down to take a closer look. Huge tracks with three toes led into the swamp.

"Those are probably dog tracks," Eddie suggested.

"Then that must be one big puppy," Liza said with a shaky voice.

Howie shook his head. "I bet those tracks belong to one of the football players," he suggested.

Eddie laughed. "I don't know any football players with three toes. Maybe the tracks belong to a three-toed purple people-eater."

"Maybe," Melody said, "the tracks be-

long to that swamp monster Eddie was joking about."

The four kids stared into the junglelike swamp. The wind rustled through the trees and above them birds screeched past. Suddenly, a shrieking sound cut through the air.

"What's that?" Liza gasped.

Melody shrugged. "I don't know, but I don't like it. Look, even the football players are leaving."

The sun had slipped behind the clouds and the football players were loading gear into their cars. "Aren't they worried about that green-haired guy?" Howie asked. "Maybe that was him shrieking."

"What if he fell in?" Liza asked, thinking about the murky swamp water.

Eddie shook his head. "That guy is a grown-up. He can take care of himself."

"I hope that whatever made those tracks isn't in there with him," Howie said softly.

"This place gives me the creeps," Liza

said. "Why don't they just bulldoze it into a parking lot?"

Melody shook her head. "If they got rid of the swamp, think of all the animals that wouldn't have a place to live."

"It's still eerie," Liza said.

All the kids nodded. Suddenly, another shriek echoed through the swamp and the kids heard a huge splash. "Quick!" Liza screamed. "Let's get out of here!"

3

Down Under

"Those footprints we saw in the park were made by a kid playing a Halloween joke," Eddie said the next morning as the four friends walked into Bailey Elementary School.

"It's almost Thanksgiving," Howie said. "It's too late for Halloween."

Melody pointed to muddy footprints in the hall. "Those aren't very funny, either," she said. "Principal Davis will have a fit when he finds out who tracked in all that mud."

"Oh, my gosh," Liza said. "Those footprints lead to our room." The kids hurried inside to find their teacher, Mrs. Jeepers, talking to the green-haired man they had seen in the park the day before.

Eddie noticed right away that the

man's shoes were covered in mud. "Students," Mrs. Jeepers said. "I would like to introduce you to Mr. Nick Bunyip. He is a visiting scientist at F.A.T.S. and he's here to talk about your ecology projects." All the kids knew about F.A.T.S., the Federal Aeronautics Technology Station, because Howie's dad worked there.

"Ecology projects?" Eddie groaned. "We have to do an ecology project?"

Mrs. Jeepers nodded at Eddie and rubbed the green brooch she wore at her neck. Most of the kids believed their teacher was a vampire. After all, she was from Transylvania and lived in a haunted house. They also thought the brooch she always wore was magical and had the power to make kids behave. Eddie sighed and closed his mouth.

"Good day," Mr. Bunyip said in a sing-songy voice.

"Hello," Liza said. "Are you from another country? You have a nice accent."

Melody nodded. "You sound like that crocodile guy on TV."

Mr. Bunyip smiled, but it didn't look like a friendly smile to Howie. "I do love crocodiles," Mr. Bunyip said. "And there are a few crocs down under, where I come from."

"Down under what?" Eddie asked. "A rock? Water? Mud?"

"'Down under' is a nickname for the country of Australia," Howie explained to Eddie.

"That's right," Mr. Bunyip said. "It's pretty quiet where I come from, with very few people. But now that's changing with cities popping up all over the place. It seems like everyone wants to build, build, build."

"That's called progress," Liza said.

"And that's why I'm here," Mr. Bunyip said. "It's my opinion that our world needs more protection and less over-crowding — especially in our world's wetlands."

13

"I agree with you," Howie said. "I'd hate to see them build a hotel on Ruby Mountain or in Bailey City Park."

Mrs. Jeepers smiled her odd little half-smile at Howie and Mr. Bunyip. "Is there anything you need for your presentation?" Mrs. Jeepers asked Mr. Bunyip.

Mr. Bunyip nodded and looked straight at Eddie. "I would give anything, and I mean anything, for a little peace and quiet."

4

Bubble Brains

That afternoon the kids headed toward Bailey City Park. They zipped up their coats against the chilly wind. "This ecology project sounds like an important assignment," Liza said. "It's going to take a lot of work."

"All homework is important," Howie pointed out.

"No, it isn't," Eddie told him. "Homework is a waste of valuable playtime."

"This is one assignment that won't waste our time," Melody said. "If we come up with a winning project, Mr. Bunyip said it could help save the environment. Our projects could really make a difference."

Liza nodded. "We have to think of

something good. Maybe I could do a poster showing the effects of dumping garbage into the ocean."

"A winning project should be more than a poster," Howie said.

"What if I showed how much land has been made into malls?" Melody said. "I could draw a map."

"A map isn't enough, either," Howie said.

"I have a winning idea," Eddie said as he kicked a soda can across the park. "I'll get the stores to donate every can of soda they have. That way I can drink them all and nobody else can throw the empty cans in the park."

Liza giggled. "You'd be so full of bubbles you'd float away."

"I think his head is already one big bubble," Howie said with a grin.

"I know!" Melody shouted. "We could all work together on a project."

Howie shook his head. "The whole

school will be doing projects," Howie reminded them. "I want mine to be the best."

"But if we worked together our project *could* be the best," Melody said. "After all, four brains are better than one."

Howie shook his head again. "I already have an idea. I'm going to ask my dad to help me set up an experiment that measures air quality in the city. Then I'll compare that to samples of air from Ruby Mountain and from Sheldon Beach."

Howie was so excited about his idea he kept talking as he walked across the field. He didn't notice that his friends had stopped paying attention. In fact, they weren't even walking with him anymore.

Howie turned around. "Hey," he said. "Where'd everybody go?"

"Shhh," Melody hissed from behind a tree. She quickly waved Howie over to their hiding place.

"What are you hiding from?" he asked.

"We're not hiding," Eddie said. "We're spying."

Howie looked where Melody pointed. Mr. Bunyip sat on a nearby bench.

"What's so interesting?" Howie asked.

"Watch," Melody said. "There's something strange about Mr. Bunyip."

Mr. Bunyip dipped a long finger into a can and licked off a big glob of tuna.

"Yuck," Liza said. "Don't they use forks in Australia?"

After he finished, Mr. Bunyip got up and carefully put his trash in a garbage can. Just then, two huge birds swooped out from behind a tree near Mr. Bunyip. He stood still, watching the birds through his green sunglasses. Then, very slowly, he started moving toward the birds.

"Mr. Bunyip looks like a cat stalking those birds," Liza said.

"Those birds are bigger than cats," Eddie said.

"Those aren't regular birds," Howie said. "They're wild turkeys. This country

19

used to be full of them until they almost became extinct. Ben Franklin even wanted to make turkeys the national bird. These woods make a perfect habitat for them."

Eddie pretended to shoot an arrow with an invisible bow. "They would make a good Thanksgiving dinner," he said.

Melody shook her head. "Those aren't the same kind of turkeys we eat at Thanksgiving," she told him.

As suddenly as they arrived, the birds took off. They swooped between nearby trees and headed toward Swamp Dread.

Mr. Bunyip watched the birds. Then with a high-pitched shriek that sent goose bumps flying across their skin, Mr. Bunyip darted after them.

"What is he doing?" Liza yelped. "He can't catch wild turkeys with his bare hands."

"It looks like he's going to try," Melody said.

"I've got to see this," Eddie said.

Before his friends could stop him,

Eddie raced after Mr. Bunyip and the turkeys.

"We can't let him go alone," Howie said. "He could get lost in the swamp."

"Serves him right," Liza said, but she followed Melody and Howie as they joined Eddie near the edge of the swamp.

"Where did Mr. Bunyip go?" Eddie asked. "He was here a minute ago, and then he just disappeared."

"He couldn't disappear into thin air," Liza told him. "We probably can't see him because the trees are in the way."

But then they heard a splash — not just any splash. They heard a huge splash.

"Or maybe," Melody said slowly, "we can't see him because he's in the swamp water!"

5

Legend

The next morning Melody waited for her friends at their favorite meeting place, under the oak tree on the school playground. Howie and Liza were the first to arrive.

As soon as Eddie jogged across the playground, Melody gathered her friends close. A few other kids played on the swing set nearby so she spoke softly, making sure no one else could hear. "I have something very important to tell you," Melody said.

"What?" Liza asked. "Are you sick?"

"No," Melody said. "This is worse than being sick." She pulled a stack of books out of her book bag. "I've been doing research."

"You're right," Eddie said as he jumped

up and grabbed a branch. "Research is much worse than being sick."

"I haven't even thought of an ecology project," Liza interrupted. "Melody, will you help me with mine?"

"I'm not doing research for an ecology project," Melody said. "I'm doing it to save Bailey City."

"What are you talking about?" Howie asked. Melody opened a book and pointed to a map of Australia.

"A map. Big deal," Eddie said, hanging upside down from the branch.

"It *is* a big deal when you hear this." Melody started reading about a legendary monster that lives in the swamps of Australia. "'Deep in Australian swamps live monsters so terrible that few who've met them lived long enough to describe them. These monsters, huge and vicious, prey on the weak. No animal or person can be considered safe from these terrible creatures, although large animals and birds are their favorite

food. When traversing the reedy swamps and lagoons, one should seek shelter as soon as one hears the monster's bone-chilling cry."

Howie reached out and grabbed Melody's shoulder. "We don't have time for fairy tales," he told her. "We should be working on our ecology projects."

"Wait. I haven't gotten to the important part. You have to hear this," Melody said. "The legendary Australian swamp monster is said to have a round head and a long neck. Don't you get it?"

"Get what?" Liza asked. "You're not making any sense."

"A round head and a long neck! That describes Mr. Bunyip!" Melody blurted.

"As well as every giraffe in the world," Liza pointed out.

Eddie jumped down from the tree. "That also describes snakes and turtles," he added.

"Well, maybe you'll believe me when

you hear what Australians call this legendary monster," Melody said. "A bunyip!"

"What are you getting at?" Howie asked.

"I think Mr. Bunyip is a swamp monster!" Melody shouted.

6

Monster Haven

Howie smiled. Liza giggled. Eddie laughed out loud. In fact, Eddie laughed so hard he had to sit on the ground.

"This is no laughing matter," Melody said. "If Mr. Bunyip is truly a swamp monster, we all could be in danger."

Liza patted Melody on the back. "You're letting Eddie's jokes about monsters get to you. Remember, there are no such things as swamp monsters."

"Even if there were," Howie said, "I'm pretty sure they don't wear green sunglasses."

"And they don't dye their hair in green spikes," Liza added.

Eddie tried to stop laughing. He snorted, gulped air, and blurted, "Every-

one knows swamp monsters don't chase wild turkeys."

"How can you be sure?" Melody said. "After all, his name is BUNYIP."

"And I know someone whose name is Frank," Eddie said, "but that doesn't make him a hot dog. Your name is Melody and that doesn't mean you're a song!"

Howie and Liza giggled. Melody didn't even smile. "You won't be laughing if I'm right," she told Eddie. "Because a swamp monster might think your name means *lunch!*"

"Why would a swamp monster show up at Bailey School to teach us about ecology?" Liza asked.

"I don't believe Mr. Bunyip is interested in ecology at all. He's interested in Swamp Dread," Melody told them.

"Who would care about that dirty place?" Liza argued.

"A swamp monster would if he needed

a place to live," Melody said. "In fact, the dirtier the better."

"Nobody likes pollution," Liza argued. "Especially Mr. Bunyip."

"Liza is right," Howie said. "If Mr. Bunyip was a monster, he wouldn't be encouraging all the kids in Bailey School to do ecology projects."

Melody put her hands on her hips. "I didn't say monsters like *pollution*," she said. "But they would like a muddy swamp that people avoid. That way they wouldn't have to worry about being hunted or about having their home invaded by hordes of people. Swamp Dread is the perfect place. No one in their right mind likes to go there."

"I like the swamp," Eddie interrupted.

"Like I said," Melody told them, "nobody in their right mind goes there. Swamp Dread would be the perfect monster haven."

"If Mr. Bunyip is really one of those

31

legendary Australian monsters, then why didn't he just stay there?" Howie asked.

"Because," Melody said, "the same thing is happening in Australia as everywhere else. Ecosystems are being destroyed by urban sprawl. As swamps disappear, the creatures that live there either die — or have to find someplace else to live. That someplace just might be Swamp Dread. If we don't do something fast, we'll be invaded by swamp monsters!"

7

The Edge of Dread

"We have to do it," Melody told her friends that day after school.

"I can't," Howie said. "I have to start on my ecology project."

Liza nodded. "Me, too."

Eddie didn't care about his project. "I'll go with you," he told Melody. "It sounds like fun."

"Okay," Melody said. "We'll meet at the edge of Swamp Dread right after supper. Bring a flashlight."

Just as the streetlights blinked on that evening, Eddie jogged up to Melody. She stood beside the football field, near Swamp Dread.

"Are you sure you want to do this at night?" Eddie asked.

Melody took a deep breath, zipped up her coat, and pulled down her cap over her ears. "Not really, but we have to prove Mr. Bunyip is a swamp monster. The only way to do it is to catch him in a swamp doing whatever it is that swamp monsters do. I've got my mom's video camera right here. Once everyone sees it with their own eyes, they'll have to believe me."

"Okay," Eddie said, switching on his flashlight. "Let's do it."

Melody and Eddie stepped carefully onto the trail's soggy soil. Their flashlights cut a narrow path through the black night air as they headed into Swamp Dread. The ground squished with each step. They had been walking for at least five minutes when they heard a gurgling sound. Eddie and Melody froze.

"What is that?" Melody hissed. "Is it the swamp monster?"

They heard it again. Only this time it was even closer.

"I think there are two monsters," Melody squeaked.

Eddie shined his flashlight in Melody's face. "Your 'monsters' are just those wild turkeys we saw yesterday. There is nothing to be scared of."

A turkey gobbled from behind a nearby tree and Melody giggled. "I guess I'm a little nervous," she admitted.

"I just hope that turkey stays close by," Eddie said.

"Why?" Melody whispered.

"Because, maybe Mr. Bunyip would rather have a turkey for dinner than us."

"You don't think a swamp monster would munch on us, do you?" Melody asked with a gulp.

"Monsters munch on anything that moves," Eddie told her. "Even kids."

"Let's hurry up and get this over with," Melody said. "Before we become a monster's midnight snack!" Melody crept toward a big tree.

Eddie shook his head. "That's the way

we came," he said. "We have to go the other way."

"Oh, no," Melody said. "Don't tell me we're lost already!"

"We're not," Eddie said, "but you are. I never get lost. Follow me."

Melody hurried after Eddie. They wound around trees, scrambled past vines, and splashed through mud. "You *are* lost, aren't you?" Melody finally asked.

Eddie turned in a complete circle. Suddenly, he held a finger to his lips. "I may not know where we are," Eddie whispered, "but I do know something is following us. Listen."

Sure enough, someone or something was behind them — and it was getting closer and closer. With the vines hanging all around them, it was hard to tell exactly where the sounds were coming from. "What should we do?" Melody squealed.

"Run!" Eddie said, but they were too late.

8

Monster at F.A.T.S.

"Why didn't you tell us you were coming last night?" Melody snapped at Liza and Howie. It was the next day and the four kids were riding their bikes to F.A.T.S., the laboratory where Howie's dad worked.

"We were worried about you," Liza said.

"You practically scared us to death by sneaking up on us in the swamp," Melody said as she pedaled up Green Street.

Eddie stood up and pedaled. "I wasn't scared," he bragged.

"It's a good thing we found you in the swamp," Howie said. "You'd probably still be lost in there if Liza and I hadn't come."

Eddie shrugged. "It would have been for nothing, anyway," he said. "We didn't

even see a swamp monster." He sounded really disappointed.

"At least I got this water sample," Melody said. "I'm hoping Howie's dad can analyze it for monsters."

The kids stopped in front of a huge building totally surrounded by a tall wire fence. Howie pushed a big button on a small post. A little black speaker erupted in static. "May I help you?" a woman's voice boomed from the box.

"I'm Howie Jones. I'm here with some friends to see my dad."

"Please follow the drive to the front door," the voice said. Slowly, the tall gates swung open. As soon as the four kids rode their bikes inside, the gates snapped shut.

A woman in a long white lab coat met the kids at the front door and took them to Howie's dad's office. Dr. Jones had a test tube in his hands. "Hi, kids," Dr. Jones said. "What can I do for you?"

"Can you help us find a monster?" Eddie said.

"What Eddie means," Melody interrupted, "is that we have some swamp water here. Could you examine it for anything strange?"

"Like monsters," Eddie said.

"We have to do an ecology project for school," Liza added.

Dr. Jones smiled. "I'd be glad to help you, but it'll take me a few minutes. Can you wait?"

The kids nodded as Dr. Jones disappeared into his lab. "We can watch through this observation window," Howie suggested. The kids looked as Dr. Jones poured the swamp water into four test tubes.

Dr. Jones dropped different chemicals into three of the test tubes. In the fourth, he placed a small blue piece of paper. "How long is this going to take?" Eddie asked. "I want to play soccer."

"Shh," Melody said. "Dr. Jones is coming."

Dr. Jones came into his office and took

off his gloves. "You kids were right," he said. "I found evidence of a monster."

"I knew it!" Melody said. "I knew there was a swamp monster!"

"I can't believe it," Liza said.

"You can believe it," Dr. Jones said. "This is the worst kind of monster — and definitely the most dangerous."

9

Monster Lagoon

"Wait until the other scientists hear about this!" Howie's father shouted. He rushed from the lab, forgetting about Howie, Melody, Eddie, and Liza.

The kids waited and waited and waited, but Dr. Jones never came back. Finally, they climbed on their bikes and pedaled away from F.A.T.S. Nobody said a word until they reached Bailey City Park. They followed the bicycle path until it reached the edge of Swamp Dread. A cold wind rattled branches. Tiny leaf tornadoes swirled out of the swamp and flew across the park. The four friends climbed off their bikes and peered deep into the shadows of the swamp.

"I knew it all along," Melody said,

pulling her jacket tight. "This place is a swamp for monsters!"

"Howie's dad didn't say that for sure," Liza pointed out.

"He didn't have to," Melody said. "It was obvious. He said Swamp Dread was the home to the worst monster ever. What could be worse than a swamp monster?"

"How about a herd of teachers?" Eddie asked as he kicked an empty can, sending it rolling along the bicycle path. "Or a passel of principals?"

"I know what's worse than a swamp monster," Liza said with a giggle. "Eddie!"

"Very funny, monster mush," Eddie said as he smashed the empty can beneath his tennis shoe.

"Stop wasting time," Melody warned. "We have to think of a way to save Bailey City."

"I didn't say anything before," Liza said softly, "but yesterday when we were looking for you, we saw a section of the swamp all cleaned up."

Melody gasped. "I bet that's where Mr. Bunyip lives. Can you find it again?"

"No," Howie said, hands on his hips. "We don't have time to go on a wild swamp monster chase. We have to work on our ecology project. It's more important."

"How can you think of homework at a time like this?" Melody asked.

"Melody has a point," Liza said. "Some things are more important than homework."

Eddie grabbed the ball cap off his head. "I agree one hundred percent. I can think of at least a million and one things that are more important than homework."

"See," Melody told Howie. "Even Eddie agrees with me."

"Eddie will do anything to get out of doing his homework," Howie argued.

"Including saving Bailey City," Melody said. "Right, Eddie?"

Eddie scratched his head and shrugged. "Sure. I'll save Bailey City from Melody's swamp monster."

"How do you plan to do that?" Howie asked.

"Easy," Eddie told him with a grin. "I'll lasso it with licorice and wrap it up with taffy. You supply the candy, I'll do the rest!"

"Stop joking," Melody said. "This monster business is serious."

"Fine," Eddie said as he kicked another soda can across the grass. It rolled to a stop next to a tree. "Do you have any better ideas?"

Melody stared at the can for a full minute. "I think Eddie just gave me the perfect idea," she said. "There's only one way to save Bailey City. We have to convince Mr. Bunyip and his swamp monster buddies that Swamp Dread isn't the peaceful haven for monsters that he believes it to be."

"And how do you plan to do that?" Liza asked.

Melody bent down and picked up a piece of paper the wind had blown against the spokes of her bike. "I have an idea," she said. "But I don't think you're going to like it!"

10

Swamp Divine

"You're right," Eddie griped on Saturday afternoon. "Your idea is worse than swamp monster snot."

Eddie, Liza, and Howie were at Melody's house. They sat in her den around a card table.

"Can you think of a better idea?" Melody asked.

Eddie scratched his elbow and thought very hard. Finally, he shook his head.

Melody held out markers and poster board. "Then get busy." She gave Howie and Liza supplies, too.

"I cannot believe I'm giving up my weekend for this," Eddie complained. "I could be playing soccer."

"I can't believe I'm doing this instead

of working on my ecology project," Howie said. "It's due on Monday."

"Maybe you'll have time to work on it Sunday night," Liza said.

Howie shook his head. "Everybody knows you're not supposed to wait until the night before an important assignment is due to get started," Howie told her.

"That's right," Eddie added with a grin. "I always start my assignments the morning they're due."

Howie shook his head sadly. Then he bent over his poster board and went to work. So did Melody, Liza, and Eddie. They didn't stop until almost dinnertime.

"Let's hope these do the trick," Melody said as the kids grabbed half of their homemade signs.

They rode their bikes around the neighborhood hanging signs on trees, light posts, and fences. The signs read:

TURN SWAMP DREAD INTO SWAMP DIVINE!

MEET AT THE PARK

FIRST THING IN THE MORNING.

"I hope this works," Liza said after they'd hung their last sign.

Melody nodded. "It will. Swamp monsters like mucky, dirty places without any people around. If we clean up all of Swamp Dread, too many people will come to enjoy it. Mr. Bunyip won't think it's the perfect place anymore. I'm sure of it."

The next morning, the kids were up early. The sky was gray with clouds and a cold wind threatened snow. That didn't stop Melody, Howie, Liza, and Eddie from meeting at the park. They weren't alone. At least twenty other kids with their parents were there.

"We came to help," said a kid with a box of garbage bags.

"This is a wonderful idea," a mom wearing a heavy pink coat added. "Swamp Dread is a dreadful mess."

Everybody worked together. They picked up trash. They collected garbage. The longer they worked, the more people joined in to help. Soon, the park was crowded with people helping to clean up Swamp Dread. The sun was high in the sky when several kids took a break.

"This place is looking much better," a boy named Huey admitted. "But how long will it last?"

"Why can't it last forever?" a tall kid named Kilmer asked.

"Because," a girl named Jane told him, "people will throw more trash around."

"Not after we hang these," Melody

said. She held up the rest of the signs the kids had made the day before. Some of the signs reminded people to pick up their trash. Other signs told about the importance of clean water, the causes of pollution, and the effects of pollution on a swamp.

"Now everyone will know how important it is to keep the swamp and the park

spick-and-span," Melody told them. "And more people will enjoy this entire area."

Everyone gathered near Melody and cheered. A few of the parents clapped.

Mr. Bunyip showed up just as they finished hanging the last of the signs. "What are all these people doing near the swamp?" he yelled. "You have ruined everything!"

11

End of the World

"We are going to be in so much trouble," Howie said, sitting on the ground underneath the oak tree. "I've never missed an assignment." It was Monday morning and their ecology projects were due.

"Maybe we could do it tonight," Liza suggested. "It would be just a little late."

Eddie dropped his backpack on the ground. "If we hadn't spent the whole weekend worrying about swamp monsters, I could have played soccer."

"Soccer isn't as important as schoolwork," Howie told Eddie. "Missing an assignment is like the end of the world."

Eddie rolled his eyes at Howie's exaggeration, but Melody shook her head. "It will be the end of our world if we don't do something about Swamp Dread and its dreadful inhabitants," she warned Howie.

"I thought we did do something," Liza said. "We got all those people to help clean up the swamp."

"I just hope it was enough," Melody said as the bell rang. The kids slowly walked into their third-grade classroom. The rest of the class carried posters and notebooks for their projects. Carey even held a glass terrarium.

Mrs. Jeepers smiled her odd little half-smile at her class. "Students, I had hoped Mr. Bunyip would be here to see your ecology projects. I am sure he would be proud."

Howie held up his hand. "Maybe we should wait until tomorrow to show our projects so Mr. Bunyip can see them," he suggested hopefully.

"How very thoughtful of you," Mrs. Jeepers said, "but we must proceed as planned. I will come down the aisles to collect your projects."

Liza gulped and Howie looked worried. They didn't want to upset their vampire teacher. Who knew what she would do? Eddie drew a spaceman on his math notebook; he was used to not having his work done on time. Melody sat up straight in her chair as Mrs. Jeepers got closer and closer.

"Melody?" Mrs. Jeepers said, stopping by Melody's desk. "Where is your project?"

"I — I — I . . ." Melody stuttered.

"Do you have a project?" Mrs. Jeepers asked, her green eyes flashing.

"Of c-c-course," Melody stammered. Melody closed her eyes as Mrs. Jeepers reached for her green brooch — the one all the kids thought was magic.

12

A Real Monster

"Our project is outside," Melody blurted.

"It is?" Eddie said in surprise.

Liza and Howie looked puzzled, but Melody nodded. "That's right. Howie, Liza, Eddie, and I did our projects together, but we have to walk over to Bailey City Park to see it."

Mrs. Jeepers frowned. "This is highly irregular, but I suppose we can take a little walk since it is such a lovely day." The kids looked out the window at the thick gray clouds.

The sun wasn't shining, but Eddie didn't care. He was happy to get outside. "Let's go!" he shouted. The kids filed outside, across the soccer fields, and down Main Street to the park.

"It's this way," Melody said. The class

stopped at the beginning of Swamp Dread. Dr. Jones and several scientists were standing there.

"Hi, Dad," Howie said to Dr. Jones. "What are you doing here?"

Dr. Jones smiled. "I might ask you the same question."

Melody spoke up. "We came to show Mrs. Jeepers how we cleaned up the park and the swamp. We even got people in the community to help us."

"We put up posters to remind people not to pollute anymore," Liza added.

"And we did it on a weekend instead of playing soccer," Eddie groaned.

"That's not all you did," Dr. Jones said. "By bringing me that water sample, I found out about the swamp monster."

"Swamp monster?" Mrs. Jeepers asked, gently touching her brooch.

Dr. Jones and the other scientists nodded. "Yes, the deadliest monster of all — pollution. And thanks to you kids, the scientists at F.A.T.S. have decided to get

rid of the water pollution in Swamp Dread."

"Hurrah!" the whole class cheered.

"I think you four have a wonderful project," Mrs. Jeepers said. "Mr. Bunyip would be very proud."

"Where is Mr. Bunyip?" a boy named Jake asked.

Mrs. Jeepers smiled her odd little half-smile. "Mr. Bunyip e-mailed me this morning that he was relocating elsewhere. He is dreadfully sad to miss seeing your projects. Now, we need to get back to class."

Melody and her friends slowly headed back to school along the edge of the swamp. Melody waited until the other kids were far ahead before talking to her friends. "See, Mr. Bunyip was a swamp monster, but once he saw all the people cleaning up this area he decided to move on. I'm sure swamp monsters don't like crowds."

"He wasn't a monster," Eddie argued.

"He was just a weird football-playing scientist. There are a lot of them around."

Liza put her hands on her hips. "Then why did Mr. Bunyip chase those wild turkeys if he wasn't a swamp monster?"

Howie shrugged. "Maybe he wanted to get an early start on Thanksgiving dinner."

"I told you those aren't like the ones we eat for Thanksgiving," Melody said. "Those turkeys are wild."

"Gobble, gobble." Eddie danced around and flapped his arms, pretending to be a wild turkey.

"Wild like Eddie," Liza giggled.

"Gobble, gobble," Eddie said. Unfortunately, he danced too close to the swamp and lost his balance. He slipped right into the mud at the edge of Swamp Dread.

"Are you okay?" Liza asked, lending a hand to help Eddie up.

Slimy mud covered Eddie from his head to his toes. Eddie wiped mud off his

arms and grumbled, "I'm fine, but Mrs. Jeepers is going to be mad."

Melody laughed. "Maybe Mr. Bunyip wasn't a swamp monster after all. But there is still one monster in Bailey City. A mud monster named Eddie!"

Debbie Dadey and Marcia Thornton Jones have fun writing together. When they both worked at an elementary school in Lexington, Kentucky, Debbie was the school librarian and Marcia was a teacher. During their lunch break in the school cafeteria, they came up with the idea of the Bailey School Kids.

Recently Debbie and her family moved to Aurora, Illinois. Marcia and her husband still live in Kentucky, where she continues to teach. How do these authors still write together? They talk on the phone and use computers and fax machines!

Learn more about Debbie and Marcia on their Web site: www.BaileyKids.com

The Adventures of
THE BAILEY SCHOOL KIDS®

❑ BAS 0-590-18983-2 **#33** Giants Don't Go Snowboarding . . . .$3.99 US
❑ BAS 0-590-18984-0 **#34** Frankenstein Doesn't Slam Hockey Pucks .$3.99 US
❑ BAS 0-590-18985-9 **#35** Trolls Don't Ride Roller Coasters . . . .$3.99 US
❑ BAS 0-590-18986-7 **#36** Wolfmen Don't Hula Dance . . . .$3.99 US
❑ BAS 0-439-04397-2 **#37** Goblins Don't Play Video Games . . . .$3.99 US
❑ BAS 0-439-04398-0 **#38** Ninjas Don't Bake Pumpkin Pie . . . .$3.99 US
❑ BAS 0-439-04399-9 **#39** Dracula Doesn't Rock and Roll . . . .$3.99 US
❑ BAS 0-439-04401-9 **#40** Sea Monsters Don't Ride Motorcycles . . . .$3.99 US
❑ BAS 0-439-04400-6 **#41** **The Bride of Frankenstein Doesn't**
                    Bake Cookies . . . .$3.99 US

❑ BAS 0-590-99552-9   Bailey School Kids Joke Book . . . .$3.50 US
❑ BAS 0-590-88134-5   **Bailey School Kids Super Special #1:**
                         Mrs. Jeepers Is Missing! . . . .$4.99 US
❑ BAS 0-590-21243-5   **Bailey School Kids Super Special #2:**
                         Mrs. Jeepers' Batty Vacation . . . .$4.99 US
❑ BAS 0-590-11712-2   **Bailey School Kids Super Special #3:**
                         Mrs. Jeepers' Secret Cave . . . .$4.99 US
❑ BAS 0-439-04396-4   **Bailey School Kids Super Special #4:**
                         Mrs. Jeepers in Outer Space . . . .$4.99 US
❑ BAS 0-439-21585-4   **Bailey School Kids Super Special #5:**
                         Mrs. Jeepers' Monster Class Trip . . . .$4.99 US

Available wherever you buy books, or use this order form

Scholastic Inc., P.O. Box 7502, Jefferson City, MO 65102

Please send me the books I have checked above. I am enclosing $_____ (please add $2.00 to cover shipping and handling). Send check or money order — no cash or C.O.D.s please.

Name _____

Address _____

City_____ State/Zip _____

Please allow four to six weeks for delivery. Offer good in the U.S. only. Sorry, mail orders are not available to residents of Canada. Prices subject to change.   BSK201